LINDSAY BARRETT GEORGE

Maggie's Ball

GREENWILLOW BOOKS
An Imprint of HarperCollinsPublishers

For Mary Maxson

Maggie's Ball. Copyright © 2010 by Lindsay Barrett George. All rights reserved. Manufactured in China. For information address HarperCollins Children's Books, a division of HarperCollins Publishers, 10 East 53rd Street, New York, NY 10022. www.harpercollinschildrens.com. Gouache was used to prepare the full-color art. The text type is Gill Sans.

Library of Congress Cataloging-in-Publication Data

George, Lindsay Barrett. Maggie's ball / by Lindsay Barrett George. p. cm. "Greenwillow Books." Summary: When Maggie the dog goes searching for her missing ball, she finds a lot of different things—including a new friend. ISBN 978-0-06-172166-3 (trade bdg.) — ISBN 978-0-06-172170-0 (lib. bdg.) [1. Dogs—Fiction.] I. Title. PZ7.G29334Mag 2010 [E]—dc22 2008052482

10 11 12 13 LEO First Edition 10 9 8 7 6 5 4 3 2 1   Greenwillow Books

Maggie is looking
for someone
to play with.

All of a sudden . . .

a mighty wind bounces her ball

Where is Maggie's ball?

Maggie decides
to look for it.

Is this Maggie's ball?

No.

Is that Maggie's ball?

No.

Is Maggie's ball up there?

No.

Is Maggie's ball here? No.

There it is, Maggie!

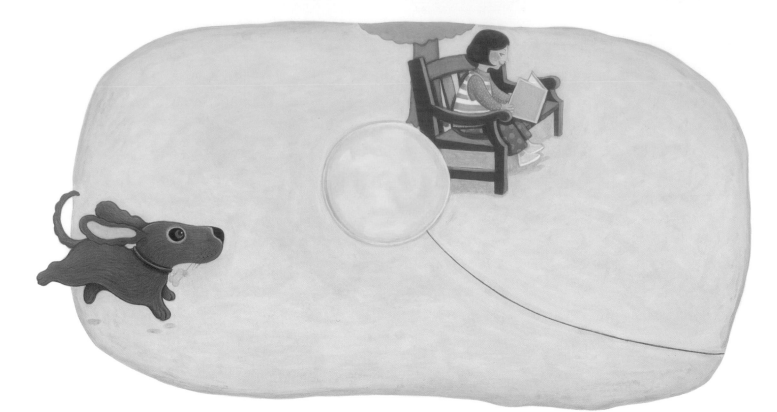

Run, Maggie!

Chase it!

Wait!
That's not a ball.

That's a balloon!

Where is Maggie's ball?

"Hello little dog.
Do you want
to play with me?"

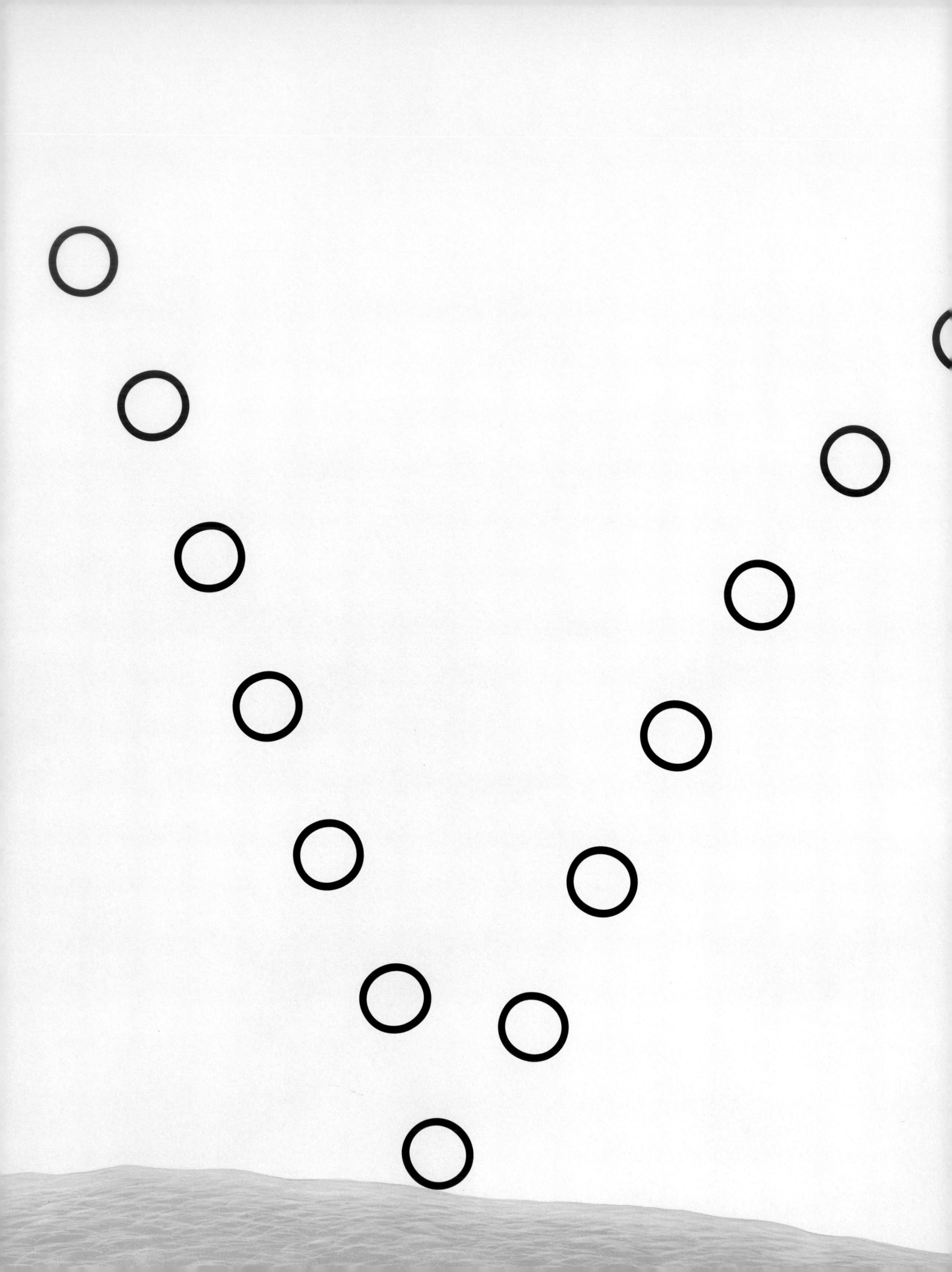

fetch!

"What a good
puppy you are."

Maggie had found
her ball.

And she
had also
found . . .

a friend.